Magic Puppy

Party Dreams

To Molly, fun little Westie run-around

GROSSET & DUNLAP
Published by the Penguin Group
Penguin Group (USA) Inc., 375 Hudson Street,
New York, New York 10014, USA
Penguin Group (Canada), 90 Eglinton Avenue East, Suite 700,
Toronto, Ontario M4P 2Y3, Canada
(a division of Pearson Penguin Canada Inc.)
Penguin Books Ltd., 80 Strand, London WC2R 0RL, England
Penguin Group Ireland, 25 St. Stephen's Green, Dublin 2, Ireland
(a division of Penguin Books Ltd.)
Penguin Group (Australia), 250 Camberwell Road,
Camberwell, Victoria 3124, Australia
(a division of Pearson Australia Group Pty. Ltd.)
Penguin Books India Pvt. Ltd., 11 Community Centre, Panchsheel Park,
New Delhi—110 017, India
Penguin Group (NZ), 67 Apollo Drive, Rosedale, North Shore 0632, New Zealand
(a division of Pearson New Zealand Ltd.)
Penguin Books (South Africa) (Pty.) Ltd., 24 Sturdee Avenue,
Rosebank, Johannesburg 2196, South Africa

Penguin Books Ltd., Registered Offices:
80 Strand, London WC2R 0RL, England

Text copyright © 2008 Sue Bentley. Illustrations copyright © 2008 Angela Swan.
Cover illustration copyright © 2008 Andrew Farley. First printed in Great Britain in 2008
by Penguin Books Ltd. First published in the United States in 2010 by Grosset & Dunlap,
a division of Penguin Young Readers Group, 345 Hudson Street, New York, New York 10014.
GROSSET & DUNLAP is a trademark of Penguin Group (USA) Inc. Printed in the U.S.A.

Library of Congress Cataloging-in-Publication Data is available.

ISBN 978-0-448-45064-3   20 19 18 17 16 15 14 13 12

Sue Bentley

Party Dreams

Illustrated by Angela Swan

Grosset & Dunlap
An Imprint of Penguin Group (USA) Inc.

Prologue

The young, silver-gray wolf bounded toward the stream that ran through the snow-covered valley. Dipping his head, Storm lapped at the clear, icy water. It felt good to be home again.

Suddenly, a terrifying howl rose in the still air.

"Shadow!" Storm gasped. The fierce lone wolf, who had attacked Storm's pack and left his mother wounded, was very close.

In an instant, there was a bright gold flash and the young, silver-gray wolf disappeared. Where Storm had been standing, there was now a tiny, spotted Dalmatian puppy with a pink muzzle, a wet, black nose, and huge, midnight blue eyes.

Storm's puppy heart beat fast and he started to tremble as he hoped this disguise would protect him. He had to find somewhere to hide—and quickly.

There was a clump of snow-covered bushes some way upstream. Storm ran toward them, almost tripping over his own paws as they skidded on the hard snow. He was just about to leap into the bushes when he saw the dark shape of an adult wolf crouching beneath them.

Storm gasped. Shadow was waiting to ambush him! It was too late to run. This was the end.

The adult wolf lifted its head.

"Storm! In here, quickly!"

"Mother!" Storm sighed with relief as he recognized the gentle face of the she-wolf.

He scrambled into the bushes, his body wriggling and his short, thin tail wagging a greeting. Canista rumbled affectionately as she licked her disguised cub's smooth, spotted fur. "It is good to see you, my son," she growled softly. "But you cannot stay. Shadow wants to lead the Moon-claw pack, but the others will not follow him while you live. It is too dangerous for you right now."

Storm growled and his midnight blue eyes sparked with anger and fear. "Shadow killed my father and three litter brothers, but he will not lead our pack. I will face him and fight him!"

Canista nodded. "One day you will, Storm. But you are still too small and I am weak from Shadow's poisoned bite and cannot help you. Use this disguise. Go back to the other world and return when you are stronger." As she stopped speaking, her eyes clouded with pain.

Storm whined with sympathy. He huffed out a puppy breath filled with tiny, gold sparks. They swirled around Canista's injured paw, before sinking into her fur and disappearing.

"Thank you. The pain is easing," Canista sighed gratefully.

Suddenly, a dark shadow fell across the bush where Storm and his mother were hiding. Iron-hard paws scrabbled at the packed snow as the fierce wolf came closer.

"Come out, Storm! Let us end this now!" Shadow challenged.

"Go! Save yourself!" Canista urged.

Storm whimpered and his big, blue eyes widened as he felt the power building inside his little body. Glittering sparks ignited in his smooth, spotted fur. The golden light around him grew brighter. And brighter . . .

Chapter
ONE

Paige Riley sat sulking in the back of her stepdad's car. It wasn't fair. She'd been right in the middle of talking about birthday parties with her two best friends, when Keith called to pick her up.

"Why couldn't Mom pick me up, like we planned? Then I could have stayed another hour with Amy and Tori," Paige complained. "Mom knows we always get excited because our birthdays all come so close together."

"I'm sorry, sweetie. I didn't want to say

anything until we were by ourselves, but your mom's been taken to the hospital," Keith explained as he pulled away from the curb. "They've done tests and she and the baby are both fine, but she's going to have to stay in the hospital and rest until he's born."

Paige was glad it was nothing serious. "Poor Mom. She hates hospitals. She won't like being stuck in there for weeks. It's a good thing spring break starts tomorrow. I'll be able to go and visit her every day and cheer her up."

Keith glanced at her in the rearview mirror. "Well, maybe not *every* day. I'm on nights for the next two weeks. So your mom and I think it's best if you stay with my mom for the time being."

Paige wrinkled her nose. She'd never met Keith's mom, but she knew that she lived in a village out in the middle of nowhere. "Do I have to? Can't I stay in town with Granny and Gramps Riley instead?" she asked.

"I'm afraid not. They're on vacation," Keith explained. "I know Brookton Village is a little remote, but I'll come over and get you when I can and take you to see your mom. By the way, try not to call my mother Gran or Nan, okay? She's a bit sensitive about her age."

"What should I call her then?"

"Her name's Deborah. She likes everyone to call her Debs," Keith said.

Paige snorted. Debs! What sort of name was that for a stepgran? "Anyway, I don't need to go and stay with anyone else. I can take care of myself in our apartment. I'm not a baby. I'll be ten in two weeks."

Keith smiled. "I know. And you're a very grown-up, sensible young lady. But

I don't like the idea of you being left
by yourself all day *and* all night. Besides,
your mom will feel happier knowing that
you'll be taken care of. We can't have
anything worrying her at a time like this,
can we?" he said reasonably.

There was no answer to that. Paige
knew when she was beaten. "But what
about my things? I need my jeans and
sneakers and—"

"I've already packed a suitcase for
you," Keith interrupted. "I can get
anything else you want later. All right?"

Paige nodded miserably, her shoulders
drooping. It wasn't all right. It was all
wrong! This new baby had somehow
managed to spoil things for her before he
was even born! She probably wouldn't

even be able to have a birthday party.

Her heart sank as she thought of Amy and Tori, who would still be planning their parties and deciding what to wear. There was no point in her joining in now.

Keith drove through town and out on to a country road. After what seemed like hours, he turned down a dark, twisty lane and stopped in front of a large, detached redbrick house. There was a light on in the porch and just as Paige reached the front door it creaked open.

A woman with tied-back, dark hair, a flowing velvet top, and jeans swooped out in a cloud of perfume. "Hello, you must be Paige. Come in, darling. I'm really looking forward to getting to know you."

Paige smiled stiffly, wishing she could say the same. "Thanks for letting me stay with you, Mrs. Stokes," she said politely.

"Oh, call me Debs—everyone does," Debs said, beaming as she ushered Paige into the house.

Paige stared at the colored floor tiles and stained-glass windows. Old-fashioned glass wall lamps cast a dim glow over the rich wallpaper and dark paintwork. The house was like something out of a creepy ghost story. Paige wouldn't have been surprised to see giant bats hanging upside down from the ceiling.

Keith took her suitcase upstairs and then came into the kitchen where Debs was filling the teapot. "I'm going to take off now. They're expecting me back at work. Will you be okay, Paige?" he asked.

Paige nodded uneasily. She wasn't okay really. She hated this gloomy house and she didn't know what to make of Debs, but she wasn't about to say so in front of everyone.

"I hope you'll be happy staying with me in my funny, old house, even though I know that you must be longing to be

at home with your gorgeous new baby
brother," Debs said, smiling warmly.

You couldn't be more wrong, Paige
thought, but she wisely stayed silent.

After Keith left, having promised to
call the following day, Debs made hot
chocolate. As they sat drinking it, Paige
stifled a yawn.

"You look worn out. This is all a bit
sudden, isn't it? Come on, I'll show you
your bedroom. Bring your drink with
you," Debs said kindly.

Paige trudged upstairs behind Debs.
Her bedroom had the same rich
wallpaper, dark paintwork, and heavy
furniture as the rest of the house. Paige
blinked at the enormous four-poster bed
that stood against one wall.

"Impressive, isn't it? That bed's been
in the family for forever. I was born in it
and so was Keith," Debs said cheerily.

Yuck! Too much information, Paige
thought. "I'd like to go to sleep now,
please," she said hurriedly.

"Of course you would, darling. It's
been a long day. Sweet dreams. I'll see

you in the morning." Debs closed the
door behind her.

Paige quickly undressed and brushed her
teeth at the big, old-fashioned sink before
climbing into the vast bed. She lay there
shivering. Moonlight poured in through
the curtains, casting shadows and making
the dark furniture into lumpish shapes.

Her tummy felt all tight and churning.
A wave of loneliness washed over her.
She wished her mom didn't have to stay
in the hospital. This was all her baby
brother's fault.

Suddenly, a dazzling flash of bright
light lit up the whole room and Paige
gasped as her sad thoughts disappeared
with the darkness. She rubbed her eyes
in disbelief—at the bottom of the bed

seemed to be sitting a tiny figure, glowing with thousands of diamond points of light.

"Aargh! A ghost!" Paige gave a strangled scream and dived under the covers.

Chapter
TWO

Paige lay under her bed covers trembling like a leaf, but nothing leaped on top of her and the room seemed strangely silent. Maybe she had imagined the whole thing. After all, she was really tired and not feeling like herself at all.

Very slowly, Paige lowered the covers and peeped over the top of them. "Oh!" she gasped.

To her complete amazement, a tiny, cute puppy with black spots on a smooth, white coat and the brightest midnight blue eyes she had ever seen was sitting on the bed.

Was it a ghost dog? Whatever it was, it wasn't glowing anymore. In fact, it was blinking at her and wagging its skinny, spotted tail. Paige found herself smiling as her heartbeat began to return to normal.

She sat up properly and leaned back
against the pillows.

"Hello! You are gorgeous! I didn't
know that Debs had a Dalmatian
puppy!" She rubbed her fingers together
encouragingly, hoping that the puppy
wanted to make friends.

To her delight, it padded up the bed
toward her and she felt its slight weight as
it climbed on to her legs.

"I am sorry if I startled you," the
puppy woofed.

Paige did a double take and snatched
back her hand. Maybe it was a ghost
puppy after all! "How come y-you can
s-speak?" she stammered.

"Where I come from, all of my pack
can speak," the puppy yapped. Despite

being so tiny, it didn't seem to be too afraid of her. "I am Storm of the Moon-claw pack. Who are you?"

Paige still couldn't believe this was really happening, but her curiosity was getting the better of her fear. She watched warily as Storm lay down on the old-fashioned bedspread and then put his head to one side as if expecting an answer.

"I'm Paige. Paige Riley. I'm staying in this spooky, old house because my mom's in the hospital resting until my baby brother's born," she found herself explaining. "My stepdad can't take care of me in our apartment because he has to work."

"I am honored to meet you, Paige," Storm woofed, bowing his head.

Paige hardly dared to move in case
she frightened this amazing puppy away.
She noticed that Storm was beginning to
tremble all over.

"Are you okay?" Paige couldn't
imagine why he might be afraid of *her*.

"I need to hide. Can you help me?"
he whined.

Paige frowned. "Who are you hiding from? Is someone after you?"

Storm's bright blue eyes flashed with anger and fear. "Yes, a fierce lone wolf called Shadow, who attacked my father and litter brothers and wounded my mother. Now he wants to lead the Moon-claw pack, but the others want me for their leader."

Paige listened in amazement. "But how can you lead a wolf pack? You're just a pup—" she began.

"I will show you!" Storm barked.

He jumped up and leaped off the bed on to the thick carpet. There was another dazzling, bright gold flash, so bright that Paige was blinded for a moment.

"Oh!" she rubbed her eyes and, when she could see again, she realized that the cute Dalmatian puppy had disappeared. In its place, there stood a magnificent, young silver-gray wolf.

Paige eyed the young wolf's sharp teeth, muscular legs, and huge paws that seemed too big for his body. As he shook himself, gold sparks danced out of his thick fur.

"Storm?" she said, inching back under the covers.

"Yes, it is me. Do not be afraid. I will not harm you," Storm rumbled in a soft growl.

But before Paige had time to get used to seeing Storm as his impressive real self, a last flare of intense gold light filled the

gloomy bedroom and Storm reappeared
before her as a helpless, little Dalmatian
puppy.

"Wow! You really are a wolf. No one
would ever guess," Paige said, deeply
impressed by Storm's disguise.

"Shadow will not be fooled if he finds
me. I need to hide now." Storm gave
a little whimper of fear as he began
trembling all over again.

Paige's soft heart went out to him. With
his smooth, spotted fur, alert, little face,
and huge, glowing blue eyes, Storm was
the most gorgeous puppy she had ever
seen.

"Why don't you jump back up here
and stay with me tonight?" she suggested.
"This bed's so enormous that half my

school could hide in it. We can think about what else to do in the morning."

Storm gave her a doggy grin and then leaped back up onto the bed, trailing gold sparks behind him like a tiny comet. "That is a good plan!"

Paige made a cozy bed for Storm by fluffing up a spare pillow.

"Thank you, Paige," Storm woofed. He jumped onto the pillow and circled around and around before finally settling down. Tucking his nose between his little, spotted front paws, he gave a contented sigh. "This is a safe place."

"Yes, but it's still very dark in here," Paige said, trying not to sound too nervous.

Storm lifted his head again. Gold

specks twinkled in his spotty fur and
a soft glow spread outward from him,
lighting up the room. "Is that better?"

"Much! Thanks, Storm." Paige lay
down and snuggled under the covers.
The four-poster bed didn't seem so big
and lonely any more.

Maybe staying with Debs in this gloomy, old house wouldn't be quite so bad now that she had Storm for a friend. As Paige and Storm fell asleep, the gentle glow filled every shadowy corner and just stopped short of spilling out under the door.

Chapter
THREE

"Rise and shine, darling!" Deborah Stokes poked her head around the bedroom door the following morning. "Goodness me. Where did that puppy come from? Keith didn't say anything about you bringing a pet!"

Paige woke instantly. She sat up, rubbing her eyes. Oh no. She must have overslept!

Storm was just waking up, too. He stretched his front paws out and yawned, showing a pink tongue and sharp, little, white teeth.

Debs put her hands on her hips. Her hair was loose on her shoulders and she was wearing a black kimono with big red poppies all over it. "I'm waiting. I think you owe me an explanation, young lady," she said sternly.

Paige gulped. "You're never going to believe this, but Storm's here because he's hiding from his evil enemy. And guess what. He can ta—" she began excitedly, but Storm suddenly reached over and tapped her cheek with one tiny, spotty front paw.

"Wroo-oof! Wroo-oof!" he said loudly, looking up at her with pleading midnight blue eyes and shaking his head.

Paige looked at Storm, confused, before realizing that the tiny puppy didn't want

30

her to tell Debs about him. She patted him reassuringly, letting him know that she understood.

"What's wrong with him? Why's he making that noise?" Debs asked, puzzled.

"Um . . . I think Storm just woke up with a bit of a jolt. He was probably in the middle of a dream or something . . ." Paige improvised hastily. She began wracking her brains for something more convincing to tell Debs that would protect Storm's secret. "Sorry, I got a bit carried away. What I meant to say was that I'm . . . er, taking care of Storm for a . . . friend. But I haven't told Mom or Keith about it. I was going to hide him in my bedroom at the apartment, but then Mom was taken to the hospital and I had to come here. Storm was in my . . . um . . . shoulder bag when Keith drove me here last night and I smuggled him upstairs. I just really want him to stay! I was going to buy dog food with my allowance," she lied.

"Hmm," Debs said doubtfully. "Why can't your friend take care of her own puppy?"

"Oh, she can . . . when . . . when she gets back from her vacation," Paige rushed on, thinking that this was getting very complicated. "But pets aren't allowed in their hotel and all the boarding kennels were full. That's why I said I'd take care of him."

Debs stood for a moment in silence before reaching out to stroke Storm. Storm looked up at her with big, dewy eyes and gave a little whine. He wagged his tail and licked her hand.

Paige had to smile at his "please-like-me-and-let-me-stay" act.

It worked. Debs's face softened. "He's certainly a cute, little puppy and he seems friendly, but I hadn't counted on having a puppy around. I'm very proud of my

garden. I really don't want him digging
up holes in my flowerbeds and burying
bones."

"Oh, he wouldn't do that!" Paige
promised. "I'll make sure Storm behaves
himself. Please say that he can stay with
me. And . . . and you won't tell Keith

about this, will you?" she asked in her best pleading voice. "I'll be grounded for at least a year!"

Debs looked at her sternly and then a big grin stole over her face. "You're a troublemaker! But I admire people who show initiative. All right, Storm can stay. And he'll be our secret."

"Really? That's fantastic! Thanks *so* much," Paige cried. "I'll take care of him really well. You'll hardly notice he's here."

Debs nodded. "See that you do," she said firmly, her eyes twinkling.

Downstairs, Debs cooked them all a breakfast of sausages, eggs, and toast. She even let Paige give Storm two sausages,

cut into tiny pieces. "But only until we get some real dog food. I don't want him being sick on my antique carpets," she commented.

Paige thought that you'd hardly notice, they were so covered in swirls and patterns, but she wisely kept silent. After

they finished eating, she took Storm into
the garden to have a little run around.

"I'm actually starting to like Debs,"
she said, wandering after him in case
any of Debs's flowers got trampled by his
little paws. "She seems strict, but she's
kind, too."

"I like her as well," Storm woofed in
agreement and then his little face turned
serious. "Thank you for not telling her
my secret. You can never tell anyone.
Promise me, Paige."

Paige felt disappointed. She thought
Storm might say this but had secretly
been hoping she could tell Amy and Tori
all about her magical new friend. They
would think this was so cool! Paige was
prepared to do whatever it took to keep

Storm safe, though. "Okay. I promise. No one's going to hear about you from me—ever!"

Storm wrinkled his little, pink muzzle and black nose, rolled his lips back, and showed his teeth. Paige blinked, worried that Storm was snarling. But he wasn't making growling noises. Why was he doing that?

Storm looked surprised at himself. He did it again. "Oh, this is how I show that

I am pleased. It is a smile. It is something special that Dalmatian dogs do," he yapped.

Paige felt a laugh bubbling up inside her, but she didn't want to hurt his feelings. Storm looked as cute as could be, sitting there practicing his Dalmatian grin.

A moment later, he shot across the lawn to chase some leaves that were whirling around in the breeze.

Paige watched him affectionately. She loved having Storm all to herself and not having to share him with anyone.

Chapter
FOUR

Keith came over to pick Paige up that afternoon before he went to the factory. "I thought you'd like to visit your mom," he said. "It might cheer her up. She's already bored with having to rest in bed."

Paige smiled. She knew that she would be.

"How are you and Debs getting along?" Keith asked anxiously as they stood in the hall.

"Fine," Paige said, shrugging. "I don't
even mind staying with her, as long as
it's not for too long."

Keith looked pleased. "I'm glad, Paige.
That'll be a big relief for your mom,
and I really think Debs is enjoying your
company."

He ruffled her short, brown hair and went to have a quick chat with Debs, while Paige went upstairs to get ready.

Paige found Storm dozing on her bed. With the autumn sunlight pouring through the window onto him, his dark spots really showed up against his smooth white fur. He opened one bright blue eye and wagged his tail as Paige bent over him.

"Will you be okay here all by yourself until I get back from town?" she asked.

Storm's other eye snapped open and he sprang up onto his paws. "I will come with you!" he woofed eagerly.

Paige smiled and stroked the top of his silky head. "I'd love you to. But what if Keith sees you? Besides, I don't think puppies are allowed in hospitals."

"I will use my magic so that no one but you will be able to see and hear me," Storm told her.

"You can make yourself invisible? Cool! There's no problem then. Maybe you should still get into my shoulder bag? You'll be safer in there until we get to the hospital."

Paige unzipped her bag and Storm jumped in and settled down on top of her woolly gloves. After brushing her hair and pulling on a fleece body warmer, Paige picked up her bag and went downstairs to where Keith was waiting.

They said good-bye to Debs and then headed for the hospital. Paige suggested they stop on the way to buy some magazines. "Mom likes the celebrity gossip ones," she told him.

"Good idea. I'll get her some flowers, too," Keith said.

At the hospital, he showed Paige down the maze of corridors to the maternity ward. Paige spotted her mom right away. She was sitting up on the second bed from the entrance.

Mrs. Riley's eyes lit up when she saw Keith and Paige. She looked flushed and pretty in a new blue nightgown and matching robe.

Paige rushed over to give her mom a hug and a kiss, delighted to see her looking well.

"Ooh, flowers *and* magazines. Lovely.

You two are spoiling me!" her mom exclaimed.

Paige sat down on the visitor's chair beside the bed. "You deserve to be spoiled, Mom. Are you okay?"

"I'm a bit tired, but that's all. I feel like a bit of a fraud staying in here actually," her mom replied. She patted her round tummy. "I'll be glad when this little man makes his appearance!"

Paige chose not to say anything. She slipped her bag off her shoulder to put it on the floor and saw Storm jump out and go rambling off down the ward. He had his head down, and his tail was wagging as he sniffed up the interesting smells. Even though Paige knew that the tiny, spotty puppy was invisible to

everyone else, she still expected a nurse
or someone to notice him. But when
nothing happened, she began to relax.
Storm was much less trouble than a baby
brother was going to be!

"I'll go and see if I can find a vase to
put these flowers in. You girls can hang
out," Keith said.

"He's being nice," Mrs. Riley
commented. "I hope it's not too awful
in that loopy, old house with Debs. She
used to be an actress, you know. And she
still dresses like one! Is she bossing you
around or anything? Just let me know
and I'll have a word with her."

Paige grinned at the determined look
on her mom's face. "Debs has actually
been really nice to me and St—" She

stopped herself quickly, realizing that
she would have to be a lot more careful
about keeping Storm's secret. "But I
don't love all her antique stuff. You
should see the monster bed I'm sleeping
in! It's as big as the entire kitchen in
our apartment!"

"Well, don't get used to having all that space to yourself," her mom said, laughing. "You'll have to go back to your ordinary, tiny, old bedroom."

"I like my bedroom being small. It's cozy," Paige said. "But I can put up with staying away from home for a little bit longer, I guess."

"Well, I'm glad you're making the best of things. Don't say anything to Keith, but I was worried that you'd feel a little lonely and cut off over in Brookton, especially since Debs doesn't have a car."

"Oh, I'll manage," Paige said. *I'm not lonely, now that I've got Storm for my friend,* she thought. She could see him sniffing around under the bed opposite them. Her lips twitched as she imagined the look on her mom's face if she knew there was an invisible puppy a few feet away!

Mrs. Riley reached out and took Paige's hand. "I'm sorry that your birthday's going to be a bit of a nonevent with me in here. Keith obviously can't manage a party with the hours he's working. You don't mind too much, do you, pet?"

Paige minded very much. She swallowed. "No problem, Mom. There's always next year," she said, trying hard to hide her disappointment.

"That's my sensible, good girl. I knew you'd understand," her mom said, fondly squeezing her hand. "Once I get home, we'll have some serious girl time all to ourselves, all right?"

Paige nodded, but she couldn't make

herself believe it. The lady in the
apartment next door had a baby. It
hardly seemed to sleep at all and when
it was awake it was crying to be fed or
changed.

A lump rose in her throat as she
wished that she could have her mom all

to herself again, like before she met Keith and before a baby half brother was on its way. Paige felt a pang as she realized that she wasn't ready to get into the big sister thing.

"Did you guys have a good chat?" Keith asked, putting the vase of flowers on top of the bedside cabinet.

Paige nodded and managed a wobbly smile. While her mom and Keith were talking, she leafed through one of her mom's magazines. Storm padded over, lay down, and rested his front paws on one of her sneakers.

"Is something wrong?" he woofed.

Paige checked that no one was listening before she replied. "I'm just feeling a little fed up, that's all," she whispered.

"Can I do anything to help?" Storm offered.

Paige shook her head. "No one can." But as she looked into his bright midnight blue eyes, she felt herself cheering up a bit. At least Storm was here just for her.

Keith dropped Paige and Storm at Debs's house and then left for work right away. There was a note from Debs in the kitchen, saying that she was at her book club at a friend's house down the road and wouldn't be long. She'd scribbled a phone number, too, if Paige needed it.

Paige got herself a drink and forked some dog food into a bowl for Storm. Storm chomped it up and then sat back, licking his chops. He trotted over to the table where Paige was sitting, staring glumly into her orange juice.

"You are very quiet, Paige," he woofed, his blue eyes clouding with concern.

Paige sighed heavily. "I was thinking about not having a birthday party this year. It's not fair. And I don't even know what to do about Amy and Tori. I know they'd understand about Mom being in the hospital. But I'd feel really weird about going to their parties, if they can't come to mine. Maybe I should just call and say that I'm not coming."

"Then your friends would be upset, too," Storm woofed.

Paige realized that he was right. "I

wouldn't want that. Okay, maybe I'll still go. Amy's is on Friday. That's only the day after tomorrow and I haven't gotten her a present yet. I should have gotten her one while I was with Keith. Now it's too late. The buses into town from here only run about once every ten years!"

Storm's midnight blue eyes lit up with purpose. "I will help. Put me down, please."

Paige did so. She frowned as she felt a strange, warm tingling sensation flowing down her spine as bright gold sparks began igniting in Storm's smooth, spotty fur.

Something very unusual was about to happen.

Chapter
FIVE

Paige watched in complete amazement as the sparks in Storm's fur grew brighter and brighter and his ears crackled and popped with electricity. A glowing, gold light spread around them both. It began forming into a long, glittery tube that suddenly whooshed through the kitchen window.

Paige stared at the shining, rainbow-shaped tube as it seemed to come to rest somewhere in the region of the town. In the middle of Debs's kitchen, there was now an entrance to a hollow tunnel. Its walls were made of millions of swirly sparks, linked together like chain mail.

"Follow me, Paige," Storm barked, leaping into the tunnel-tube.

"Wait for me!" Paige called a second later, dashing after him.

The magic tunnel was springy underfoot and the walls rippled, bouncing Paige along, so that in no time at all she suddenly shot out with a loud *pop!* Storm sat on the pavement, waiting for her.

"Oh! That was fantastic!" Paige gasped, swaying slightly. Her legs felt quite wobbly—just like she'd been on a bouncy castle!

She looked around and saw that she and Storm were now in a quiet alleyway behind some wheelie bins. Paige realized where they were. There was a big shopping center just around the corner.

"Now you can buy Amy a present," Storm woofed, looking pleased with himself.

Paige quickly bent down to stroke him. "Thanks, Storm."

She didn't waste any time, as they had to get back before Debs returned and noticed they were both gone. Paige hurried into a big store and went straight to the toy department. Amy was crazy about fairies and had tons of fairy books. She even had a string of fairy lights around her wall mirror.

Paige chose a fairy doll with a lavender dress and crown and matching glittery wings. "Perfect! Isn't she pretty?" she whispered to Storm. "Do I have time to get a card?"

"Yes, but you will have to hurry. This sort of magic does not last long," Storm barked softly.

Paige set off again, but upon reaching the card department she stared in dismay. "There're about a hundred million cards here. I don't know which one to choose."

Storm waved one tiny front paw and a shower of golden glitter shot out. From out of the corner of her eye, Paige noticed a fairy-shaped card glowing as brightly as a star on one of the racks. As she picked it up and opened it, tinkling fairy music played "Happy Birthday."

"Yay! Amy will love this!" Paige went and paid and then hurried outside into the alleyway after the little puppy.

The golden tube began to fade as Paige got close. There was no time to waste. She and Storm plunged in and, once again, Paige felt the tunnel's springy walls and floor helping them along.

Suddenly, the tube began to ripple much faster than before and Paige and Storm went shooting forward.

"Oof!" she cried as, with a loud burping noise, the tunnel spat them both out and they landed on their bottoms

on the kitchen floor. The tunnel began
to dissolve into fizzing sparks before
disappearing with a final loud *pop!*

Paige gingerly picked herself up and
grinned. "That was so much fun and I've
got an amazing present for Amy. Thank
you, Storm!"

The tiny puppy's little muzzle wrinkled
in his cute Dalmatian grin. "I am glad I
was able to help."

Paige had barely caught her breath
when the kitchen door swung open and
Debs came in.

"Hello, darling. Discussing all those
books has made me hungry. I think it's
time for dinner. Have you and Storm
been having a good time?" she asked.

"Er . . . yeah!" Paige said, winking at

the tiny puppy. *You'd never believe me,
even if I told you*, she thought.

On Friday, Debs insisted on booking
a taxi, so Paige and Storm arrived in
style at Amy's house. Storm was invisible
to save Paige having to offer awkward
explanations.

"Happy Birthday!" Paige gave Amy her
card and present.

Tori stood by as Amy unwrapped it.
"Oh, I absolutely love her!" Amy said
delightedly, clutching her lavender fairy
doll. "How did you know?"

"Know what?" Paige asked, puzzled.

Amy and Tori exchanged knowing
glances. "Come and see!" They practically
hauled Paige into the kitchen.

Paige's eyes widened as she saw the
pink tablecloth strewn with sequins,
the plates of dainty food, and the big
birthday cake in the shape of a fairy
castle. There were sparkly pink and violet
streamers trailing down the walls.

"It's a *total* fairy party! Don't you just
love it?" Amy said.

"Wow! It looks . . . magical!" Paige
said delightedly.

They played Pin the Wing on the
Fairy. Everyone fell down laughing when
Amy's dad pinned the wing on the
fairy's nose. There was Pass the Magic
Parcel and then a dressing-up game with
cardboard, tinsel, and colored tissue and
a prize for the best fairy costume. Tori
won it easily.

"Wait until you see what we're doing at *my* party," Tori said to Paige. "It's going to be very grown-up. Fairies are okay, but they're a little babyish, aren't they?" she said, flicking back her long hair.

"Amy doesn't seem to think so. Neither do I," Paige replied. "Aren't you having fun?"

"Well—yes," Tori admitted.

"What are you complaining about then?" Paige joked, giving her a friendly dig in the ribs.

Tori laughed. "It's so great that our birthdays are so close together, isn't it? We're the Party Girls!" she said, doing a twirl.

Not this year, Paige thought sadly,

but she didn't want to spoil the happy mood by saying anything yet.

When no one was watching, Paige gave Storm some party treats. He sat on the window sill, enjoying watching the party without being trampled on. "I like party food," he woofed happily, chomping his fairy-sized sandwiches and chips.

When Paige's taxi arrived to take her home, Amy's mom handed her a pink, satin goody bag. Paige said her thank yous and good-byes and Amy and Tori waved from the doorstep. "See you at my party on Monday!" Tori called.

Storm sat on Paige's lap in the back of the taxi. "I don't mind going back to Debs's too much. I'm starting to like her," Paige sighed, stroking his soft,

spotty fur. "But it feels mega-wrong
not to have a party. Especially as me,
Amy, and Tori have spent forever talking
about it."

Storm whined sympathetically.

Debs was waiting eagerly at the door
to let Paige and Storm in. "Tell me
everything and don't leave anything out!
What did your friends say when they
saw Storm? Did you tell them you were
taking care of a puppy?"

"Um, yes. They made a big fuss over
Storm," Paige said. She quickly changed
the subject. "Amy's party had a fairy
theme. It looked so pretty . . ." she said.

Debs listened as Paige told her about
the games and the yummy party food.
"I've been thinking," she said when

Paige had finished. "It's a shame that you can't celebrate your birthday properly with your mom in the hospital. How would you like a tea party here, for you, Amy, and Tori?"

"Really?" Paige said, surprised. She

didn't have the heart to tell Debs that she'd been looking forward to something a bit more special. A tea party didn't sound all that exciting. "Thanks very much. That would be . . . very nice."

Debs beamed. "That's settled then."

Chapter
SIX

The next time Keith took Paige and
Storm to the hospital to visit her mom,
she made sure she asked him to take her
shopping afterward.

"Okay then. But I'm in a bit of a rush.
Do you know which store you need?"
Keith said.

Paige nodded. She knew just what Tori
wanted. She bought her a CD of her
favorite boy band, a pack of colored gel
pens, and a card in the shape of a shiny
designer handbag. "And can we just stop

back at the apartment? I want to get some clothes. I'll be super-quick!" she pleaded.

Keith drove to their block and sat outside with the engine running, while Paige dashed up the stairs and along the concrete walkway. Storm followed Paige into her bedroom and flopped down on her fluffy floor cushion while she burrowed in the wardrobe.

"I like this place," he woofed, looking around at the bright posters on the walls.

"Me too! It's tiny but it's all mine," Paige said, stuffing a blue top with a sparkly butterfly and her newest jeans into her bag. It felt comforting being back home among her snow globes, framed pictures, and old Barbie dolls. She couldn't resist picking up the battered, old teddy who always sat on her bed and giving him a cuddle.

When it was time to go, she had to wrench herself away. She sighed sadly as she shouldered her bag and quickly locked the front door. "I wish I didn't have to go back to Debs. I can't wait

until Mom comes home and we can be a family again," she said to Storm as they hurried back down to where Keith was waiting.

Only now, it'll be a different kind of family, she thought worriedly. *One with a tiny, smelly, fussy baby that demands everyone's attention.*

On Monday night, Paige dressed in her sparkly butterfly top and jeans.

"Oh, you look so pretty. Wait a minute, I've got just the thing to go with that outfit," Debs said.

Paige made a face. "Oh no. She's probably going to bring me one of her flowing velvet jackets," she whispered to Storm.

"Is that a bad thing?" Storm woofed softly, looking puzzled.

"Er . . . yes!" Paige said. "I can't go out looking like a pair of curtains!"

But Debs returned with a pair of cool clip-on earrings, the same color blue as Paige's top. Paige put them on. "Oh,

I love them! Thanks, Debs. They're perfect."

Debs looked pleased. "Would you like me to do your hair? I've got a set of heated rollers somewhere."

Paige was thinking how to refuse politely, not wanting to push her luck, when Amy and her mom arrived to pick her up.

"Have a good time," Debs called as Paige walked down the front garden. "Oh, just a minute. Didn't you forget something? Storm!"

Paige froze. Storm was walking invisibly at her ankles. Debs obviously couldn't see him, so she thought Paige had left him behind. Turning around, she ran back toward Debs. "I left him in my room. He seemed a bit tired," she said, hoping Debs wouldn't go upstairs to check.

"What was all that about?" Amy asked as Paige got into the backseat of the car and sat next to her. "She said something about a storm."

"Um . . . yes. She thought it might rain later . . ." Paige said vaguely. "Anyway, let's not worry about that. We've got Tori's brother Dean to worry about instead. Yuck! I hope he isn't at the party—he's so annoying."

"You can say that again," Amy said.

"He's so annoying," Paige repeated and they both laughed.

When they arrived at Tori's house, Paige spotted a tall, thin boy with dark hair and a pimply face. "Oh great.

There's Dean," she whispered to Storm. "Look out for him. He can be a real nuisance with his nasty jokes."

Storm showed his teeth in a tiny growl. "That is not a good way to act."

Amy, Paige, and Storm wandered into the bright, shiny kitchen and gave Tori her presents. There was a big display of expensive gifts on a sideboard. "Those are all mine. Aren't I lucky?" Tori said proudly.

"Well, you are our bestest, sweetest big girl," her mom cooed, giving her a hug.

Dean pretended to stick his finger in his mouth and made gagging movements. For once, Paige didn't blame him. But then he spoiled it by hanging around and making stupid comments while Tori

opened her presents. "Felt tips! Bor-ring.
You're ten, not six, aren't you?" he
hooted, when she opened Paige's.

Paige blushed hotly, as she felt Storm
nudge her leg protectively with his wet,
little nose.

Tori just giggled. "They're gel pens
actually. Just what I wanted. And this
CD is great. Thanks, Paige."

"That's okay," Paige said, glaring at
Dean and wishing he'd go away.

Dean made a face at her and walked
out of the kitchen.

"This way, everyone!" Tori cried,
leading the way into the living room.

The two enormous leather sofas had
been pushed back and a shiny covering
placed over the carpet to make a dance

floor. A stack of disco equipment with big speakers stood near a row of lights flashing different colors.

Paige and Amy were seriously impressed. "Wow! It's just like a real club!" Amy said.

Tori smiled proudly. "I *told* you I was having a grown-up party. I'll put the CD Paige bought on my new player and we can do our routine to it."

Paige felt self-conscious with everyone watching. But she soon relaxed and remembered all the steps. Everyone clapped when they finished.

Storm barked excitedly, too, but only Paige could hear him. She winked at him when no one was looking.

The dancing was so much fun, until Dean joined in. He jumped around, knocking into people on purpose.

"Ow!" Paige cried, when he leaped on her foot. "Now who's acting like a six-year-old!" she muttered.

Dean's face darkened as he heard her.

"Listen, everyone! Paige's in a rage! I'm really scared," he mocked.

"You're so pathetic," Paige said disgustedly, turning her back.

Tori's dad made fruit-juice cocktails with colored ice cubes and little umbrellas. He handed them out on a tray, like a real waiter. "Food's ready, when you're finished dancing," he announced.

Storm followed Paige outside to the supersized barbecue. His little, black nose twitched at the delicious smells wafting toward him. "That human food smells good," he woofed.

Paige smiled at him. "Knowing Tori's parents, there'll be millions of expensive sausages and top-notch burgers. You'll love them."

Everyone trooped over to the tables and chairs on the lawn. Storm sat under Paige's table. She slipped him some meat, but he found plenty to chomp up from all the bits the others dropped. It was all Paige could do not to giggle. He was better than a vacuum cleaner!

"My party's the best in the whole world, isn't it? Wait until you see my cake. It's got three layers *and* sugar roses. The bottom's chocolate, the middle's lemon, and the top's strawberry. It's amazing," Tori said.

Paige fought down a stab of anxiety. Debs's tea party idea was looking more pale and pathetic by the moment. Maybe she should just tell Debs that she didn't want a party after all. Amy and Tori were going to be so disappointed with a boring, old tea party.

Paige shook her head sadly as Tori's mom lit the candles on the amazing birthday cake and everyone sang "Happy Birthday." Paige took a plate when the multicolored slices were passed around, but she didn't feel very hungry anymore.

Soon afterward, parents began arriving to pick up their kids.

"Mom will be here for us soon. I'm going to get my coat," Amy said.

"Okay," Paige replied. She decided that she'd better fetch Storm. The last time she'd seen him, he was exploring the bottom of the garden.

But Paige couldn't find him. He definitely wasn't nosing about in any of the flower beds. Suddenly, a loud yelp of fear came from the direction of the tree house.

Paige gasped as she caught sight of the tiny, spotted puppy wobbling on a branch, high above the ground!

Chapter
SEVEN

Paige's pulse raced as she ran toward the tree.

"Come back here, you stupid mutt!" a voice called angrily and Paige saw Dean leaning out of the tree-house window, reaching for the trembling puppy.

Paige realized that Storm must have been so scared that he'd forgotten to make himself invisible. He couldn't use his magic to help himself now that Dean could see him.

"Hang on, Storm!" Paige cried as

she leaped forward. Suddenly, Storm's paws slipped and his back legs swung in midair. His tiny legs scrabbled for a foothold and then he whimpered as he felt himself falling.

Paige's heart missed a beat. She

stretched out her arms and just managed to catch Storm, but she was still rushing forward. With the tiny puppy in her arms, she couldn't put out her hands to stop herself and crashed into the tree trunk with a massive *thud*.

Paige fell to the ground, dazed.

"Oh, flipping heck!" Dean cried. He ducked inside the tree house and began climbing down.

Paige felt a familiar prickling sensation down her spine as bright gold sparks bloomed in Storm's spotty fur and his little, black nose glowed like a gold nugget. Storm leaned close and very gently touched her chin with the tip of his wet nose.

A warm, fizzing feeling spread outward

from Paige's chin. It washed over her face
and forehead and then trickled down over
the back of her neck. In just a second, she
felt as clearheaded as if she'd just eaten a
very strong peppermint.

She sat up with Storm still in her lap.

Dean appeared beside them, just as the
very last spark faded from Storm's coat.

"You're sitting up! I thought you—" he
said in a panicky voice.

"We're fine. No thanks to you!" Paige
fumed, losing her temper. "What sort
of person tries to scare a tiny puppy,
especially high up in a tree!"

"I didn't mean to scare him!" Dean
snapped, flushing. "I was just messing
around." His eyes narrowed. "How come
you know its name, anyway? Is it yours? I

didn't see you with it at the party."

Paige hesitated. "I've . . . um . . . seen Storm around here before. He must live with one of your neighbors."

"Funny. I've never seen him," Dean said suspiciously. "I'll come with you to take him back."

"No! I mean, I can do it by myself," Paige insisted, but her heart sank as she saw the determined look on Dean's face.

As Dean took a step toward Paige, Storm lifted his lip and growled softly. He leaped out of her lap and ran behind the tree.

Paige felt another faint tingling sensation down her spine. A little spurt of gold sparks puffed up from a nearby pile of grass cuttings and vegetable peelings.

Suddenly, there was a strong gust of
breeze, which blew the entire heap
toward Dean.

Whoosh! A cascade of compost swept
him off his feet. *Splop!* It covered Dean
up to his neck and held him firmly to the
ground. "Help!" he croaked, spitting out
shreds of brownish leaves.

Paige left him there. "You'd better
stay invisible now. Come on, Amy's
mom's probably here to pick us up,"

she whispered to Storm as they hurried back toward the house. "What you did to Dean was a bit mean," she scolded gently. "But he deserved it!"

Storm's bright blue eyes glowed with mischief. He wrinkled his muzzle in a cute Dalmatian grin. "Perhaps it will teach that mean boy a lesson. My magic will wear off in a few minutes."

Paige laughed. "I'd give two weeks' allowance to see him trying to explain how a compost heap attacked him! Brothers definitely seem like a real pain."

Storm put his head to one side. "But having a baby brother might be different. He would be little and helpless and it would be someone to look after," he woofed softly.

"Maybe," Paige said, not convinced.

She felt a surge of affection for the tiny puppy. She knew that Storm meant well and didn't want to hurt his feelings by disagreeing. But she was still very far from being happy about having to share her mom with the baby.

A couple of evenings later, Paige and Debs sat on the dark blue velvet sofa with Storm curled up between them. They were watching a late-night movie on TV about some kids who got trapped in a haunted house.

"I'm not sure your mom would approve. Maybe we should switch channels before this film gives you nightmares," Debs said, reaching for the remote.

"Oh, I watch much worse stuff than this," Paige lied. She felt very grown-up, staying up late and eating popcorn with Debs. Besides, nothing could scare her while she was cuddled up with Storm!

She reached down to stroke his smooth, warm, little body. On the TV, a door in the haunted house creaked open, revealing a four-poster bed and heavy furniture. Storm pricked up his ears and sat straight.

"Groof!" he barked, pawing Paige's arm excitedly. "Why is your bedroom in that box with moving pictures?"

Paige grinned. It did look just like her bedroom. She'd always thought this house was the perfect setting for a creepy film!

An amazing idea for a birthday party jumped into her mind. She was dying to

tell Storm about it now, but she didn't
dare to risk it with Debs sitting so close.

As soon as the film finished, Paige
jumped up and went into the kitchen to
make Debs a cup of tea. She piled some
biscuits onto a plate and brought them
back in with the tea. She saw that Storm

wasn't on the sofa and decided to go and look for him after she'd spoken to Debs.

"Ooh, lovely. Thanks," Debs said, taking a sip of tea. "What have I done to deserve this? Are you after something, young lady?" she joked.

Paige felt herself blushing. "Well . . . actually, I did want to talk to you about my . . . um . . . birthday tea party," she said sheepishly.

Debs dunked a ginger nut. "Fire away then. I'm all ears."

"I was wondering if Tori and Amy could stay the night. Instead of a tea party, maybe we could have a midnight feast. We could easily all sleep in my bed. I thought we could read ghost stories and play creepy games. It could be a scary sleepover. What do you think?" she asked.

Debs nodded thoughtfully and beamed at Paige. "You clever, old thing, you! I wish I'd thought of it. It's a great idea. I've got some old Halloween decorations in the attic and we could put some candles in glass jam jars. I'll dress up and be your spooky waitress, if you'd like. How about if I made dead man's hands, skeleton biscuits, and blood tablets for the midnight feast?" she said, getting into the swing of things.

"Ooh, yes! That would be fantastic!" Paige cried delightedly. "Can I help make them?"

"Of course you can. That's half the fun. There's a bus into town tomorrow.

We can go shopping, if you'd like. I was going to ask if you wanted to come with me and choose a present. And we could stop and visit your mom if we've got time. What do you think?"

"Yay! Thanks, Debs. You're the best!" Paige threw her arms around Debs and hugged her. She couldn't wait to find Storm and tell him her exciting news.

Chapter
EIGHT

Paige skipped upstairs, expecting to see the tiny puppy curled up on her bed, but he was nowhere in sight. "Storm?" she said, looking around the room.

She checked under the pillows and covers and then looked under the bed and in the wardrobe. But there was still no sign of Storm. Paige finally found him underneath the old-fashioned dressing table, curled into a tight ball against the wall.

"Oh, I get it. We're playing hide-and-seek—" Paige began and then her face changed as she saw that the tiny puppy was trembling. "What's wrong? Are you sick?"

Storm shook his head, his midnight blue eyes troubled. "I sensed that Shadow was close and I heard dogs growling in the street outside the house. I think he has set them on to me," he whimpered.

Paige felt a stir of alarm, but she hadn't heard anything with the TV on. She went and peered through a crack in the curtains, but the street below was empty. "There aren't any dogs there now," she told him. "How will I know they're Shadow's dogs if they come back?"

Storm lifted his head. "They will be

ordinary dogs, with fierce, pale eyes and extra-long, sharp teeth. Shadow's magic will make any dog I meet into my enemy now."

"Then we'll have to make sure that you keep well hidden," Paige said. She managed to reach right underneath the dressing table with one hand and stroke Storm reassuringly.

The terrified puppy slowly uncurled

and finally crept out with his belly brushing against the carpet. Paige picked him up and gently tucked him into bed. "There, you're safe now. I hope that horrible Shadow will keep right on going and fall into the sea! Then you can stay with me forever and live in our apartment," she said.

Storm peeped over the covers, his little face serious. "I cannot do that. One day I must return to my own world and the Moon-claw pack. Do you understand that, Paige?" he woofed.

Paige nodded sadly but she didn't want to think about that now. She loved having Storm all to herself. Climbing onto the bed, she curled herself around Storm.

"I've just been talking to Debs. I've got some great news about my party . . ."

Paige grinned at the squeals of delight coming out of the phone the following day when she told Amy and Tori about her party. They were both at Tori's house listening to CDs.

"A scary sleepover is so cool!" Amy said.

"Yes. Almost as good as my party," Tori said.

"See you both on Saturday! And remember to bring your PJs." Paige hung up the phone before turning to Storm. "I'm going into town with Debs now. I'd love you to come with us, but I'm worried about Shadow finding you."

"I am, too," Storm barked, his bright eyes flickering with fear. "You go with Debs and I will stay here and hide."

"Okay then, if you're sure. See you later. We'll bring you back a treat," Paige promised.

Although she had a lovely day with Debs in town, she couldn't help feeling anxious. What if Storm's enemies came back? He might have to leave without even saying good-bye. The thought of Storm leaving made her realize how much she adored her magical friend. She felt determined to enjoy every precious moment with him.

"Would you like something to wear for your birthday?" Debs asked. They were on the way back to the bus

stop with bulging shopping bags and had
stopped outside a clothing store.

"Okay," Paige said, hiding her impatience
for Debs's sake. Inside the store, she ran

up to the first rack and grabbed a black
and silver top in her size. "Can I have this,
please?"

Debs raised her eyebrows. "Don't you
want to try it on?"

"No. This size fits me fine. I love it. It's
just right for my sleepover."

"All right. If you're sure," Debs said. She
paid for the top and they set off for the bus.

It was only half an hour later, but to
Paige it felt like hours before the bus
dropped them at the bottom of the lane
in Brookton. The moment they got in the
house, she dumped her shopping bag in the
kitchen and shot upstairs.

"I need to go to the bathroom!" she
shouted over her shoulder at a surprised
Debs.

As soon as she went into the bedroom, Paige saw Storm's little, spotty tail sticking out from under one of the pillows. "I'm back. Storm!" she crooned happily, gently uncovering him. She picked him up and cuddled him, breathing in his clean puppy smell. "I'm so glad that you're still here! My scary sleepover party wouldn't be any fun without you."

"I am looking forward to that very much," Storm yapped, his pink tongue darting out as he covered her chin and nose in warm, little licks.

"Happy birthday, sweetie!" Mrs. Riley said, handing Paige her card and presents.

As Paige opened them, her face lit up. She had some new sneakers, a Hunt the

Monster board game, and a gift card for
downloading music. "Wow! Thanks.
These are amazing!" she said, hugging her
mom and then Keith.

Storm sat beneath the visitor's chair. As
there'd been no more sign of any enemy
dogs, he and Paige had decided that it
was safe for him to come, too.

At the end of visiting time, Paige kissed her mom. Paige thought she looked a bit pale. "Are you okay?" she asked her.

"Yes, fine. Your brother's a bit restless, that's all."

Paige remembered what Storm had said to her about having a new little brother. It did sound like he needed someone to take care of him. Paige decided that she'd think about it some more later on.

"Have a lovely sleepover party, darling. And I wouldn't mind a slice of birthday cake!" her mom said.

"I'll bring you one tomorrow. Bye!" Paige sang out.

Chapter
NINE

Paige and Debs got to work right
away, getting things ready for the party.
Paige helped decorate gingerbread men
biscuits with black-and-white icing for
skeletons. The blood tablets turned out to
be tiny strawberry-jam sandwiches. But
the dead man's hands were her favorites.

"These are dead clever. Dead, get it!"
Paige joked, filling clear plastic food
gloves with popcorn, before tying the
ends and dipping the finger tips into pink
icing.

Debs laughed. "That's a truly terrible joke."

Paige smiled at Storm, who was "helping" by crunching up any bits of popcorn that escaped. Time seemed to fly and Paige had to run upstairs to get changed.

She had just thrown on her new black and silver top, when the doorbell rang. Paige came downstairs, with Storm at her heels to let her friends in.

Amy beamed at Storm as he wagged his tail in a friendly fashion. "Oh, what a cute puppy! Is he yours?" she said, fussing over him.

Tori bent down to stroke Storm, too. "Was he a present for your birthday? You never said you were getting a puppy. What's his name?"

"Storm," Paige said. "He's . . . er . . . not mine. I'm just taking care of him for someone while I'm staying here. Debs has been great about it."

"Did someone mention my name?" called a deep, hollow voice. Debs glided into the hall, wearing flowing black clothes. Her face was milk white and her mouth was a slash of red. "I am Paige's witchy godmother and I am at your service for tonight! This way, please!"

Paige was impressed. Debs was very convincing. She must have been a really good actress.

Amy and Tori's eyes widened in delight when they saw the party food. The dead man's hands were a huge

success. The birthday cake was an extra
surprise from Debs. It was shaped into
a monster face, with sugared jelly-worm
hair, a liquorice nose and eyebrows, and
gobstopper eyeballs.

Debs made a magic potion by scooping ice cream into glasses of cola before handing them out.

Paige loved her presents. Amy's was a comedy DVD called *Revenge of the Monster Moles*. Tori had bought her an expensive-looking notebook and matching folder and some sparkly hair pins.

"Your chamber is ready, young ladies, if you'd like to follow me upstairs," Debs said in her spooky voice.

"I can't wait to see their faces when they see my room," Paige whispered to Storm.

Plastic bats and spiders hung from the ceiling. Red and black streamers and fake spider webs decorated the bed, and candles glowed from inside jam jars on the window sill.

"I can*not* believe that bed!" Tori jumped on to it and lay spread out like a starfish. "Come on. Let's get our PJs on!"

They all changed and got into bed. Even with three girls and a puppy in the bed, there was still tons of room. Storm curled up on the pillow next to Paige. Tori and Amy made a huge fuss over him.

"I wish I had a puppy like yours," Tori crooned. "I'm going to make my mom and dad buy me one exactly like Storm," she decided.

Paige bit back a grin. "I think they'd have a hard time finding a puppy like him. Storm's one of a kind," she said, smiling fondly at him.

Tori looked a teeny bit annoyed. "He's not the only Dalmatian puppy in the world, you know," she said huffily.

"You're so lucky, Paige," Amy said. "Debs is great and you can stay in this amazing house whenever you like. And you're going to have a sweet, little baby brother soon."

"I wish I had a younger brother or sister. I'd love to cuddle a baby and take it for walks in its stroller," Tori sighed.

Paige hadn't considered it like that. Maybe Amy and Tori were right. She'd thought her friends were the lucky ones and now it seemed like they envied her.

Tori suddenly grinned. "Anyway," she said, changing the subject. "I thought this was supposed to be a scary sleepover.

I haven't exactly been scared of anything yet."

Paige saw Storm dive under the bedclothes and then felt a familiar prickling sensation. What was he up to?

"Whoooo! Whoooo!" A loud noise wailed suddenly. All the spiders, bats, and ghost shapes leaped off the walls and zoomed toward the end of the bed, where they hovered in the air before shooting back into place.

"Argh!" Tori screamed delightedly. "That was fantastic. How did you do it?"

"Sound effects and . . . er . . . hidden wires," Paige said, winking at Storm as he reappeared and snuggled up next to her.

"This is the best party ever," Amy exclaimed.

"Until mine, next year . . . what?" Tori said as Paige and Amy grabbed a pillow each and battered her.

They made a pact to stay up all night, but after playing Paige's Hunt the Monster game and giggling for an hour as they swapped silly jokes, they snuggled down together. Amy and Tori went to sleep first.

"Good night, Storm," Paige whispered, her eyelids drooping.

"Good night, Paige," Storm woofed, sighing contentedly.

Paige's eyes snapped open. A noise somewhere outside the house had woken

her. She reached for Storm, but there
was only a tiny, warm place next to her
where the puppy had been.

Paige crept quietly out of bed, so that
she didn't wake Tori and Amy, and

tiptoed out on to the dark landing. From the window, she could see two fierce dogs sniffing around in the front garden. Moonlight glinted on their pale eyes and extra-sharp teeth.

Paige gasped. Shadow's dogs! Storm was in terrible danger. The moment she had been dreading was here. Her heart pounded as she knew she was going to have to be strong for Storm's sake.

Suddenly, a bright flash of gold light streamed out from the open bathroom door at the far end of the landing. Paige threw herself forward and rushed inside.

Storm stood there, a tiny, spotty puppy no longer, but a majestic, young, silver-gray wolf with a glittering neck-ruff. An older she-wolf with a gentle face stood next to him.

Tears pricked Paige's eyes. "Your enemies are here! Save yourself, Storm!" she burst out.

Storm's big, midnight blue eyes narrowed with affection. "You have been a true friend, Paige. Be of good heart," he said in a velvety growl.

"I'll never forget you, Storm," Paige said, her voice catching.

There was a final dazzling flash and big, gold sparks filled the bathroom, floated down around Paige, and crackled as they hit the floor. Storm and his mother faded and then were gone.

A furious snarling sounded outside in the front garden, but then all was silent.

Paige stood there, still stunned by how

fast it had all happened. Her heart ached, but she was glad that she'd had a chance to say good-bye to her magical friend. She knew that she would always remember the time she'd spent with him.

She looked up with tears in her eyes to see Debs standing there. "Paige? Did the telephone wake you up? Keith just called. You've got a beautiful baby brother. He was born a few minutes ago. Apparently

he's got the most amazing dark blue
eyes."

Just like Storm, Paige thought, with
a sense of wonder. She had a sudden
thought. "What time is it?" she asked.

"About ten minutes to midnight," Debs
told her.

Her little brother had been born on her
birthday! She was a big sister now. Paige
felt an unexpected warmth flood through
her at the thought of meeting her
tiny, helpless, brand-new little brother.
Wherever he was, she knew that Storm
was smiling in approval.

About the Author

Sue Bentley's books for children often include animals or fairies. She lives in Northampton and enjoys reading, going to the movies, and sitting watching the frogs and newts in her garden pond. If she hadn't been a writer, she would probably have been a skydiver or a brain surgeon. The main reason she writes is that she can drink pots and pots of tea while she's typing. She has met and owned many cats and dogs and each one has brought a special kind of magic to her life.